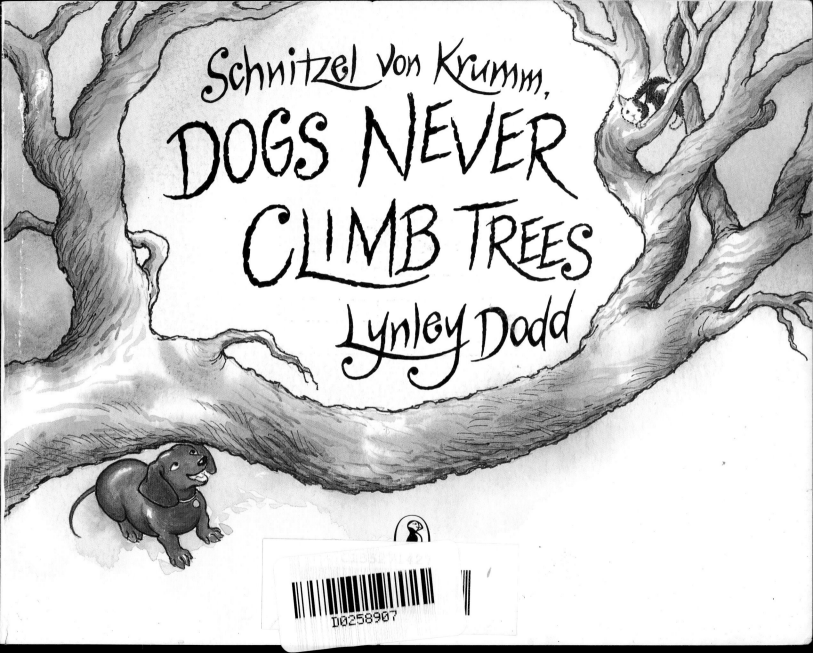

Schnitzel von Krumm, DOGS NEVER CLIMB TREES

Lynley Dodd

A dog to remember
is Schnitzel von Krumm,
with his very short legs
and his very low tum.
He can bury a bone
in a minute or two —
there are MANY
remarkable things
he can
do.

He can hide in a woodpile
of branches and twigs,
and he disappears
into the holes
that he digs.

He fetches the paper,
his rug and his bowl —
sometimes his fetching
gets out of control.

He can hustle and tease
with the greatest of ease,
but everyone knows that
dogs
NEVER
climb
trees.

He can gallop and scamper
round bushes and bends —
he has to run fast
to keep up with his friends.

He scatters the birds
when they're taking a bath,
and sloshes the water
all over the path.

He can hustle and tease
with the greatest of ease,
but everyone knows that
dogs
NEVER
climb
trees.

He can ride on a skateboard.
He teeters on top
and flies through the air
when it comes to a
STOP.

His nose is so certain,
his sniffer so sound,
he can rustle a rabbit
from deep in the ground.

He can roll in the mud,
he can wallow and play
till he changes from brown
to a globulous grey.

He can hustle and tease
with the greatest of ease,
but everyone knows that
dogs
NEVER
climb
trees.

BUT
if they are bold
and adventurous too . . .

it might just be possible . . .

maybe . . .

they DO!

PUFFIN BOOKS

Published by the Penguin Group
Penguin Books Ltd, 80 Strand, London WC2R 0RL, England
Penguin Group (USA), Inc., 375 Hudson Street, New York, New York 10014, USA
Penguin Books Australia Ltd, 250 Camberwell Road, Camberwell, Victoria 3124, Australia
Penguin Books Canada Ltd, 10 Alcorn Avenue, Toronto, Ontario, Canada M4V 3B2
Penguin Books India (P) Ltd, 11 Community Centre, Panchsheel Park, New Delhi – 110 017, India
Penguin Group (NZ), cnr Airborne and Rosedale Roads, Albany, Auckland 1310, New Zealand
Penguin Books (South Africa) (Pty) Ltd, 24 Sturdee Avenue, Rosebank 2196, South Africa

Penguin Books Ltd, Registered Offices: 80 Strand, London WC2R 0RL, England

puffinbooks.com

First published in New Zealand by Mallinson Rendel Publishers Ltd 2002
Published in Puffin Books 2003
10

British Library Cataloguing in Publication Data
A CIP catalogue record for this book is available from the British Library

ISBN-13: 978-0-14056-943-8